© Copyright 2007 Tracie Choates
All rights reserved. No part of this publication may be reproduced, stored in a retrieval system, or transmitted, in any form or by any means, electronic, mechanical, photocopying, recording, or otherwise, without the written prior permission of the author.

Note for Librarians: A cataloguing record for this book is available from Library and Archives Canada at www.collectionscanada.ca/amicus/index-e.html
ISBN 1-4251-1385-0

Printed in Victoria, BC, Canada. Printed on paper with minimum 30% recycled fibre.
Trafford's print shop runs on "green energy" from solar, wind and other environmentally-friendly power sources.

Offices in Canada, USA, Ireland and UK

Book sales for North America and international:
Trafford Publishing, 6E–2333 Government St.,
Victoria, BC V8T 4P4 CANADA
phone 250 383 6864 (toll-free 1 888 232 4444)
fax 250 383 6804; email to orders@trafford.com

Book sales in Europe:
Trafford Publishing (UK) Limited, 9 Park End Street, 2nd Floor
Oxford, UK OX1 1HH UNITED KINGDOM
phone +44 (0)1865 722 113 (local rate 0845 230 9601)
facsimile +44 (0)1865 722 868; info.uk@trafford.com

Order online at:
trafford.com/06-3144

10 9 8 7 6 5 4 3 2

This is a work of fiction. Names, characters, places, and incidents either are the product of the author's imagination or are used fictitiously, and any resemblance to actual persons living or dead, events, or locales is entirely coincidental.

PLAYING THE

GAME AS A

MAN!

Tracie Choates

http://www.traciechoates.com

To my husband, Reggie and my son Marcus,

my parents, David and Connie,

and my brother Jason.

Thank you for constantly believing in me.

Acknowledgements

I want to take this time to say thank you for the love and support of all of my family and friends.

For I know none of this would be possible without the love of God on my side.

I would like to give a special thanks to some close friends, Chandra, Gina, Connie, Catrina, Alma and Catrese, these girlfriends have shown nothing but love and respect over the many years we have known each other. They have always wished me the very best in life. I thank them now and always.

Dear Reader,

I would like to share a very inspirational story told in an exciting way. It's very quick, easy to read and simple to follow.

Have you ever been fired or laid off from a job or know somebody that has? Do you have any kids or know somebody that does?

Do you like at least one reality game show?

Have you ever been treated unfairly in your place of work or know someone that has? Do you have a dream? Do you believe in Love? Then this book is for you. Yes-you.

Find out all the comical things that happen when Tina gets close to her dream.

How far would you go to make your dream a reality?

Chapter One

Dear Tony,

It's 2:00 o'clock in the morning, and I can't do anything but think about you as the rain drops tap against my window. With every couple of drops I have flash backs into our past. I only have good memories. Memories of us always getting along, never fighting. Since you lived right next door, we would stay up for hours just talking about life. It didn't matter what the topic was, I remember we always had good conversation. You made me feel safe. I know that seems crazy to say since we were only teenagers, but you did. I don't think anybody knew you like I did; you were always a perfect gentleman. I remember at times I'd wish you really weren't so predictable. You did get one in on me, I surely didn't predict that kiss, nor will I ever forget it. I remember how you looked into my eyes, I started to get nervous and you whispered two words to me, "I Know" Just those two words alone made me feel like you did understand me, and we were on the same page; just one week after that I quickly realized that we weren't. I remember thinking, "he's not what I need. I need excitement, fun, unpredictable living." You went back to treating me with the utmost respect. Not to say that you didn't before, it was just very predictable and somewhat boring. You controlled your emotions and feelings very well. You never once after that just let your guard down and had fun. I could tell that you really cared about me; as a matter of fact anybody who knew us could look at us and see that same thing. It was an unspoken love. At the time I think we didn't know what to do with it, so we did what most teenagers wouldn't do in our situation, absolutely nothing. We could go on and think of people to blame for us missing out on several years of a wonderful life we could have had up to this point. But we really only have ourselves to blame. Then we still don't really know how things would have turned out. I always said, I only have one life to live, and I don't know when my time is going to be up, so I try and live life to the fullest. You know, trying new things, going new places, just trying to see and do everything I haven't yet experienced.

*With all of that said, I know you're not proud of what you saw on T.V.
I was greedy and selfish to go after my dream in the manner in which I
did; dressing up as a man on national television, and exposing young
children to such behavior. I know this isn't the type of behavior you
would expect from me. And probably wouldn't want to be associated
with someone who did such crazy things just to see a dream come true.
I know I let my controlling, independent ways get out of control.
Hopefully, you can find it in your heart to forgive me and at least pick
back up where we left off.*

*I know this may sound crazy, but you haven't returned my phone calls
so that's why I'm sending you this email. Please read the attachment
I'm sending, it's a movie script of all this craziness that's been going
on over the past month. A screenwriter/ producer came over and
wanted to make my story into a movie, and since you are part of the
story, I just wanted to get your opinion. I'm really hoping that you will
forgive me. It's real simple to follow, and not very long. Please email
me back once you've finished reading it.*

FADE IN:

INT. TINA'S WORK BUILDING — DAY

It's loud, phones ringing, people yelling,
swearing and laughing. TINA is a very beautiful
and sexy Network Administrator with a spicy
personality. She walks through the Help Desk
department to get a cup of coffee, in the break
room.

                    ANALSYT 1
              (squeezing a stress ball)
No, it's no problem at all-I know it's been 3
hours... just click on...

                    ANALYST 2
     (trying not to laugh while he reads the man's
                  sexy e-mails)
Sir that's what happens, when you
visit the porn sites... I'll help you clean...

                    ANALYST 3
    (pushing the mute button, while swearing back
                at the customer)
I apologize that we've caused you to lose so
much business today...but no, I can't...

                    ANALYST 4
Sure, go ahead and put your eight year old on
the phone... I'm sure he does...

                    ANALYST 5
So the one person you are sending mail
to, can't open it? Well maybe it's...

Tina walks back through the help desk from the break room, after getting her coffee. She stops and talks to some of the Analysts on her way.

                    TINA (to Analyst 1)
You need to get Grandma off the phone, just get her IP address and take over.

Tina walks to the next analyst.

                    TINA (to Analyst 2)
Tell the pervert, tough luck- he's got to do a complete reinstall of all his software.

Tina walks over to her girlfriend the receptionist. SARA is very petite with a big colorful personality.

                    SARA
Word is- they are going to fire somebody today.

                    TINA
Really, these analysts don't know how to handle these customers.

                    TINA
All they do is lie. Knowing they down loaded something or just installed something that messed their computer up. But when you ask them they swear they didn't do anything, I remember when...

                              CUT TO:

8

INT. CALL CENTER BUILDING - DAY (Flashback)
1997

In a classroom, Tina is standing in front of
the class with the INSTRUCTOR.
The Instructor look's stressed out from
handling to many escalations from customers.
Her hair is pulled back in a pony tail. She's
wearing large hoop ear rings, shirt with the
company's logo, and tan khakis.

                INSTRUCTOR
Let's do some scenarios, I'll be the caller.

                INSTRUCTOR (angry)
Hey! I just bought this DAMN PC and my
monitor is broke!

                TINA (quietly)
I'll give you an R-A number to return it.

                INSTRUCTOR
Oh! Hell-NAW! You give the customers too much
credit. You must assume the customer is dumb,
lying or really dumb! Finally, you must take
control of the call. Let's try it again.

                INSTRUCTOR
Hey I just spent $3,000 dollars on this PC, and
the monitor is broke!

                TINA
Did you try plugging the DAMN thing in!

                INSTRUCTOR (laughing)
YES! You've got it. You assumed the dumb factor
and took control of the call. If not, they will
assume you are dumb, even though they called
you for help.

BACK TO SCENE

                SARA
Soon you'll have your own Call Center, right?

                TINA (walking away)
Yeah, supporting the development of my own
Operating System; I'll give *Microsoft* a real
run for their money. I have to go check my
messages before the meeting. See you later.

INT. TINA'S OFFICE - DAY

Wall filled with all of her Technical Awards
and Achievements. Picture of her with the first
PC she built. The single most import picture is
a detailed designed of her building for the
Call Center. The building is shaped into a
cylinder form with the building rotating
directly in the center of the building with the
name DYNO on the top.

Tina walks in, sits down, and plays her voice
mail on the speaker phone.

                LADY (voice on machine)
Tina, this is Bank of US, to complete your
business loan approval you must be able to
bring $30,000 to the table in 30 days. Have a
great day!

                TINA
$30,000, where am I going to get $30,000?

Sara walks in Tina's office.

                SARA
Girl, see that's why you need a man... you in
here talking to yourself. See if you had a man,
you could talk to him and maybe have a kid or
two.

                TINA
Girl, you know I barely have time for myself,
let alone time for some insecure, stubborn,
overworked man, who produces bad kids.

TINA'S OFFICE BUILDING — BOARD ROOM- DAY

Tina's boss JOE, and co-worker TOM and other
co-workers are present at this meeting. Tom is
very sly, a kiss up in everyway, and does what
it takes to get recognition for the smallest
things. They all are sitting at a rectangle
table with the boss sitting at the head; and
TOM sitting by his right side. JOE is a very
rigid man, speaks direct and to the point.

Tina walks in. She sits on the left side of the
table at the end; the other three men are
sitting very quietly.

                TINA (sits down)
Good morning everybody.

                JOE
Sorry team, but we have to make
some cuts because of the Merger.

11

                    TINA
What?! When was this decided?

                    JOE
Last night.

                    TINA
When will it take place?

                    JOE (looks at his watch)
Four minutes and counting.

                    TINA
What? This has got to be a joke,
Where are the camera's, am I getting *PUNKED*?

                    TOM (interrupting)
Sir, I've been dedicated to the company for 10
years.

                    TINA
I've been dedicated for nine years.

                    TOM
I'm productive, I save the company money.
                    TINA
I'm productive, and have my B.S. in Computer
Science, Certified with Networks.

                    TOM
Sir, I built this network, laid down
cables and all, with a Master's Degree.

                    JOE
What I need right now is a good
team player to remain with us.

TOM (pulls out a disk)
Sir, I have built a great rapport with
all of our employees, if I may sir, show you.
He puts in the disk and plays it. It's a
commercial of him promoting the Computer
Olympics Games. He's one of the creator's of
the program. It ends.

TINA
What? What is that? Kids, that has nothing to
do with us, anybody can teach a kid to be a
team player.

TOM (pulls out a new disk)
You're right. May I, sir?

He puts in the new disk. It shows testimonials
of analysts and his other team mates, saying
what a great team player he is all the time. It
ends.

TINA (to Joe)
When did you say you found out about the cuts?

JOE
Tina, I'm sorry-- but you're fired!

TINA
What?! Hey, what is this *THE APPRENTICE?*

JOE (yells)
Security!

TINA
What about my things?

Joe points to the door, she opens it and all her things are in a little tiny box with her name pre-printed on a label.

Chapter Two

TINA'S HOUSE - DAY
Sara comes over Tina's house, and lets
herself inside of her house.

                SARA (clapping her hands)
Come on sleepy head, get up!

                TINA (rolls out of bed)
Do I have to actually start looking
today? It shouldn't be that hard.

                SARA (opens her blinds)
Come on, you know what they say-

                TINA (rubs her eyes)
But who are "they" Sara who are "they"?

Sara walks to the bathroom and turns on the
shower.

                SARA (O.S.)
                (yells)
The early bird catches the worm!

                TINA (yells back)
All right, all right! Who was it
that said you could have a key to my house?

                SARA (walks back to bedroom)
You know that one man you had over last week?

                TINA
What? What Man!

                SARA (looking in her closet)
My point exactly! When you get one I'll give
him the key. Hey, I found something for you to
wear.

Tina walks to the bathroom and starts to get in
the shower.

                SARA (O.S.)
                (yells)
I'll check on you later, Bye!

INT. TINA'S HOUSE - DAY

Tina is getting dressed while watching
television.

                TOM (voice on TV)
So parent's, don't forget to have your kids
take the test online at www.
kidscomputerolympics.com, so that he or she
might have the chance to be on my team at the
next Computer Olympics.

                TOM (voice on TV)
I can help get your kids prepared for the real
world of Computers and how to be a great team
player at the same time!

Tina turns off the television, and walks to the
computer. She starts to surf the Internet for
jobs.

                    TINA
Okay, *Careerbuilder*, *Monster*, *Computer Job
Store*-Hook me up!

She starts to submit her resume to several
positions.

                                        CUT TO:

Six hours later, she's still sitting in the
same chair, and 10 empty bottles of *Mountain
Dew's CODE Red* all on the floor. Suddenly she
gets up and runs to the bathroom. She starts to
urinate.

A full minute later, she's still peeing. The
phone rings. She tries to hurry while still
urinating, by jumping up and down and spreading
her legs wider. After she finishes, she jumps
up and tackles the phone, hits the speaker
button.

                    TINA (very calmly)
Hello?

                    LADY (on phone)
Yes, Hi I'm a loan specialist
just wondering if you-

                    TINA
WHAT? No...NO!

                    LADY (on phone)
Would like to take this opportunity
to consolidate your student loans?

She hangs up the phone.

INT. TINA'S HOUSE - DAY - ONE WEEK LATER
(FLASH FORWARD)

Tina is talking on the phone pacing the floor.
She is fully dressed in her interview suit with
black heels and hair styled neatly.

                TINA (into the phone)
I know but if I want the job-

                TINA (frustrated)
Over qualified? Thanks.

INT. TINA'S HOUSE - DAY- TWO WEEKS LATER (FLASH
FORWORD)

Tina is pacing the floor. She is fully dressed
in her interview suit with fuzzy slippers on,
and hair styled neatly.

                TINA (into phone)
I'll take the pay cut.

                TINA (into phone)
Over qualified? Thanks.

INT. TINA'S HOUSE-DAY— THREE WEEKS LATER (FLASH
FORWARD)

Tina has on jeans and a t-shirt and tennis
shoes.

                    TINA (into phone)
Yes, is this the manager of *McDonald's*?
I was thinking about a career change.

                    MANAGER (O.S.)
Come on down, if you are a Team player.

                    TINA (into phone)
Team player! Just to say, "Would you
like that number four super-sized?!"

She hangs up, and the phone rings back
immediately.

                    TINA
Hello...

                    TINA
Help Desk! I haven't work on a help desk in
years... $8.50hr.

                    TINA
Pay rate? It was $35.00hr. I guess
it's $8.50hr now. See you then.

She hangs up the phone.

Chapter Three

INT. CALL CENTER — ALPHARETTA, GA - DAY

Tina sitting taking calls. Signs are posted,
"Be patient", "Let the customer hear your
smile" "Show Empathy".

> TINA
> (playing solitaire)
> Yes, do as it says, press
> any key Ma'am, A-S-D-F any one...

> CUSTOMER (on the phone)
> But, I don't see the ANYKEY!

> TINA
> Just press the DAMN return key!

Tina is still sitting taking calls. Other signs
posted," Stay within support boundaries" "No
gross abuse"

> TINA (into phone)
> (still playing solitaire)
> No. I said, "What Operating System
> are you working with?"- Internet Explorer is a
> browser. How could you not understand that?

> TINA
> Just click yes, to that question "are you sure
> you want to delete it?"

Tina still taking calls; other signs posted, "Always, Always show how much you care no matter what!"

                    TINA
Sir, I can't help you with your printer problem, that's not our problem, call the manufacturer- Dummy.

                    CUSTOMER
I heard that!

                    TINA
Good! Pass it on!

Manager comes over to her cubicle and places his hand out for her headset. Tina hands it to him.

                    TINA
I guess the QA team heard that one, huh?

                    MANAGER
We hear and see everything! Even when you were on *Craig's List* looking for other jobs! By the way, Good Luck!

                    TINA
Whatever, I'm out, like I need this little job.

She's escorted out the building.

                              CUT TO:

21

EXT. TINA CAR - DAY

Tina is talking on her cell phone while
driving.

                    TINA
Girl, I needed that little job!

                    TINA
Please come over later and help me
figure something out, I have to come up
with $30,000 in a week for my software
company.

INT. BUILDING DOWNTOWN ATLANTA - DAY

Sara is in a design and makeup class. She's
putting makeup on one of the students.

                    SARA
Okay girl, I'll be over later, don't panic!

INT. TINA'S HOUSE — NIGHT

Tina fell asleep waiting for Sara. Her body is
sitting upright in the chair, at her computer
desk with one hand on the keyboard and one hand
on the mouse. Sara never showed.

Chapter Four

EXT. PHILIPS ARENA BUILDING - DOWNTOWN ATLANTA - DAY

People are lined-up outside the building, loud music, lights, and TV networks. On the top of the building, there are huge balloons depicting kids of all nationalities, holding hands, standing in front of a super large ballooned computer. On the computer screen it reads, "Computer Olympics" in white.

The REPORTER is very clean, and nicely groomed, he is interviewing the applicants standing in line. He walks up to Tina.

> REPORTER
>
> So, you're here today to see if you can be one of the team leads in the next the Computer Olympics.

> TINA
>
> Wow! Did you figure that out all by yourself?

> REPORTER
>
> Well, this is the 5th Annual Computer Olympics held in Atlanta, GA under the Direction of Tom White. This event is nationally televised.

> REPORTER
>
> The leader of the winning team gets $30,000. The kids receive a free computer and a Scholarship for $40,000 dollars to the college of their choice.

                    REPORTER
Now, these aren't high school kids, these kids
are between the ages of 10 and 12. That's 5th
and 7th graders. They have the opportunity to
have their future set before going to high
school.

                    REPORTER
The kids qualified by taking a computer test
with over 500 questions on it. The adults to
lead the teams also have to take a test; it's
going to be a long day, with over 6,000
applicants down here. Back to you JIM!

JIM is a news reporter back at the station. The
one thing that stands out about JIM is he wears
a blonde hair piece, that doesn't match the
rest of his hair.

                                    CUT TO:

INT. NEWSROOM - DAY

                    JIM
There you have it! Who will be the next
Computer Olympic Champions; you will be able to
watch the games live next week right here on
Channel 5 at 6:00pm.

BACK TO SCENE

Tom, her ex-coworker is at the door greeting
the applicant's. Tina walks inside the door.

                    TOM (to Tina)
What do you want?

                    TINA
A JOB of course!

                    TOM (laughing)
You honestly think that I would give you
a job. A job here, working with me?

                    TINA
Why not?!

                    TOM
What!? You don't know the first thing
about being a team player, nor anything about
kids.

                    TINA
How do you get time to do this?

                    TOM
I get a special Leave of Absence, for the
summers.

                    TOM
I remember when you could have helped
but you didn't, like when...

                                    CUT TO:

INT. CALL CENTER BUILDING - DAY
(FLASHBACK) 1998

Joe, Tom and Tina are in a room looking at 300
large computer boxes, stacked very high.

                    JOE
As you see, the new computers
came in for the help desk.

                    TOM
Yes Sir, when should this be completed?

                    JOE
No later than, end of business, today.

Joe walks out of the room. Tina phone rings.

                    TINA (into the phone)
What! Reschedule. I have to come now?

Four hours later. Tina walks back in the room
with her hair and nails looking
fabulous. Tom has almost completed the work,
he's buried underneath all the empty boxes.
Tina picks up a computer.
Their boss Joe walks in.

                    JOE
Great Job! Great team work!

Joe quickly walks out. Tom tries to fight his
way through all the empty boxes, tripping and
falling all over his self. He SCREAMS out.

                    TOM
What? Wait a minute! Team work, my ASS!

BACK TO SCENE

                    TINA
Are you going to hold that against me? I was in
a wedding. I had to get my hair
and nails done.

                    TOM
Yes. I developed some bad paper cuts from that.

Tom shows his hands to her; cuts are
everywhere.

                    TINA (trying not to laugh)
WOW! It looks like you tried to shake hands
with *Edward Scissor Hands*.

                    TOM
You think that's funny.
We'll see who has the last laugh.

                    TINA
So, can I apply for the job?

                    TOM
No! Go try your team player skills
somewhere else.

                    TINA
I already did. Besides, I really
need the money for my business.

                    TOM (laughs loud)
Now that's funny!

                    TOM (shouts)
Next!

A man in the line steps in front of her, and
bumps her out of the way. She gets pushed into
a tall dark very well groomed man, DAVID. She
looks up in amazement.

                    TINA
Oh-um, excuse me.

                    DAVID
Don't worry about it, its kind-of rough
down here today.

                    TINA
Are you part of the Games?

                    DAVID
Me, no I'm the Tech support for the
equipment here on the set. How about you, are
you going to try your luck with the test?

                    TINA
There is kind-of ummm...little problem with
that.

                    DAVID
I'm sure you are the kind of lady that when you
see something you want, you go after it.

                    TINA
Yes, I am. What about you? You always go after
what it is you want?

                    DAVID
No, unfortunately, I don't. I believe if it was
meant to be, it will work out.

                    TINA
Well me, I can't rely on chance.

Tina starts to walk away and waves goodbye to David. She pulls her phone out of her purse and calls her girlfriend Sara. She stands in a corner.

          TINA (whispers)
Girl, you have got to meet me at my house.

                           CUT TO:

INT. SARA AT WORK - DAY

          SARA
What?! When...? Why?

EXT. PHILIPS ARENA BUILDING - DOWNTOWN ATLANTA, GA - DAY

          TINA
Now! Please... Did you take your lunch?

INT. SARA AT WORK — DAY

          SARA (eating at her desk)
No, but-

EXT. PHILIPS ARENA BUILDING - DOWNTOWN ATLANTA - DAY

          TINA (into phone)
Okay, meet me there and bring your makeup case.

Chapter Five

```
INT. TINA'S HOUSE - DAY

Tina is standing in front of the mirror dressed
in a Men's Black Pinstripe suit, with black
shiny shoes. She has on a male short blonde
wig, with black framed glasses on, with blue
contacts in her eyes. She also added some
padding to look fat.


          TINA
Can you tell it's me?

          SARA
Yeah right, not with all that white makeup on,
but where did you get that suit?

          TINA
Goodwill! I picked it up on the way.
But seriously, do I look okay?


          SARA
If I was a girl into white chubby guys, I would
date you.


          TINA
I just want to be sure that Tom,
doesn't recognize me when I go back down
there to apply for the job.

          TINA
I've got to get that money for my business.
```

SARA
I don't know the rules, but I'm pretty
sure they don't want people pretending
to be another race and gender.

TINA
I'll deal with that, when I have to.

SARA
I'm just saying you're shaping the minds of
young impressionable kids.

TINA
What? I'm not worried about them kids, I need
my money, plus I ran into this cute guy down
there. And it wouldn't hurt to run into him
again.

SARA
But you are a guy now, a white guy, at that!

TINA (she puts on a tie)
Yeah-yeah, I'll worry about that later.
How does my tie look?

SARA
It's pink. What can I say?

TINA
A lot of guys are wearing pink now.

SARA
Good luck! I've got to get back to work.

TINA
Hey, promise me you will make me one of those
fat suit things if I pull this off.

                    SARA
Sure, why not, drag me into this even more.
Hey, maybe I can use this experience to prove
my skills.

                    TINA
Right, most definitely! We can do this.

INT. PHILIPS ARENA DOWNTOWN — DAY

Tina is now taking the test in a clear sound
proof booth. She has to answer 100 questions
in 30 minutes and get 98 questions right.

Every time she gets one right a green button
lights up and displays the number correct on
the outside of the booth. She is now up to 96
correct and one wrong.

                    TINA (V.O.)
I can do this- I can do this! (BUZZ)

She answers one more wrong.

                    TINA (V.O.)
I can't do this- I can't do it!

MAN in the crowd yells.

                    MAN
He can't do it!

                    TINA (V.O.)
Concentrate. Business...business...

She answers one more right. (DING)

>   TINA (V.O.)
Money! Money!

She answers one more right. (DING)

The News Reporter starts filming her while she's attempting to answer the last question.

>   REPORTER
Folks, yes we are still down here at the try outs for the leaders for the Computer Olympic Games. Only one spot remains open, but it could be filled in just moments.

She starts to sweat; the makeup on her hands starts dripping on the keys of the keyboard.

>   TINA (V.O.)
One more, I can do this.

>   REPORTER
Maybe, he can't do it.

>   TINA (V.O.)
Concentrate. Business, Money-

David the Tech walks by.

>   TINA (V.O.)
And him! (DING-DING-DING)

She gets the last one correct. The crowd goes
wild. CHEERING and hooting and yelling.

She steps out of the booth and steps down in
front of David.

                DAVID
Congratulations, Man.

Tina shakes his hand, and white makeup comes
off onto David's hand.

                TINA (voice deepens)
MAN, Oh yeah, thanks!

                DAVID
I'll come around later and show you around the
set.

                TINA
Maybe we can even hang out or something.

Tom walks up and introduces his self to Tina.

                TOM
Hello, I'm Tom. I'm one of the creator's of
this program, and also a contestant with an
unbeatable team this year.

                TINA
Really, that remains to be seen, wouldn't you
say?

She pauses for a second.

                    TINA
How can you be a contestant and creator, that
don't seem fair?

                    TOM
First, no, I will win. And secondly, the money
that I win is donated to a charity. Just
promise, you won't scream like a girl when I
win.

                    TINA
As long as you, promise the same thing.

          TOM (shakes Tina's hand)
Deal.

Tom notices the white powder but doesn't know
what it is. He wipes it on his pants in
disgust.

Chapter Six

MONTAGE - TINA AND SARA GO SHOPPING IN ATLANTA
FOR MEN CLOTHES.

--Tina and Sara are in a dressing room trying
on different suits, the sales lady looks
confused, but accepts that maybe that they are
gay.

--Tina is getting dressed in another men's
store and a guy winks at her as he comes out,
and gives her his card with his personal number
on it.

--Sara and Tina are at another men's store
trying on men shoes, and Sara is trying to
teach her how to walk like a man, but looks
funny doing it.

MONTAGE - TINA AND SARA - MAKING THE FAT SUIT.

--Sara and Tina are at Tina's house. Sara is
making the mold of Tina legs and arms.

--Sara and Tina hours later are still at Tina's
house. Sara is now making the fat mold and
applying the color to it.

-- Tina and Sara still at the house. Sara
finishes and Tina tries on the fat suit. She
starts to play in it. Rolling and jumping,
making the fat roll around in different
directions.

INT. PHILIPS ARENA DOWNTOWN ATLANTA - NIGHT

50 thousand kids cheering and clapping. Tina
and Tom are facing each other behind podiums.
Tom has three identical triplet boys on his
team. And Tina has two girls and one boy.

Lights and introduction starts for the Game
Host. GEEKY AL comes running out on stage.
GEEKY AL looks the part. He has long black
hair, pulled back in a pony tail. He's wearing
tan pants, and loafers, with a white button
down shirt; also wearing black framed glasses.

                GEEKY AL
Hey boys and girls! Are you ready for a Crazy
and wild show? When I say Computer, You say
Geek! Computer!!!

                AUDIENCE
Geek!!!

                GEEKY AL
Computer!!!

                AUDIENCE
Geek!!!

                GEEKY AL (chuckles)
Gosh! Thanks you guys for introducing
yourselves.

                GEEKY AL
Geeks of America, lets get to know
the geeks that have been chosen to play this
year's Computer Olympics.

Audience cheers very loud. The news camera's
are rolling.

                    GEEKY AL
The team lead on the RED team is Tom the
returning Champ of five years in a row. He must
a Big Geek! Oh, did I say the out loud?

Audience cheers very loud.

                    GEEKY AL (runs to RED Team)
Red Team, let's get some introductions.

Geeky Al puts the microphone in front of the
first kid. HERMAN is wearing tan pants black
framed glasses, with spiked hair.

                    GEEKY AL
Fellow geek, give us your name, age, and actual
time of birth... just kidding. All we really
need is your time of birth. Okay, still
kidding.

                    HERMAN
My name is Herman, I'm 12 years old, I'm from
New York.

                    GEEKY AL (interrupting)
Herman, we didn't ask you for all that, since
you gave additional information we will have to
deduct 20 points from your score. Just kidding-
just kidding!

GEEKY AL moves on to the next kid on the RED team, SHERMAN he is also wearing tan pants and black frame glasses, with spiked hair.

                    GEEKY AL
Same drill and spill!

                    SHERMAN
My name is Sherman, and Herman is my twin brother and I'm 12 years old.

Audience laughs.

                    GEEKY AL (smiling)
Dude, I think your brother gave your age away.

Geeky Al walks on to next brother, VERMAN, also wearing tan pants and has spiked hair.

                    GEEKY AL
Let me guess, your name is Berrrrman, and you are 12 years old.

                    VERMAN
No, my name is Verman! You Geek!

                    GEEKY AL
Gotcha! Verm- Verminator.
Wow, how does your mother tell you guys a part?

Herman, Sherman, and Verman turn around and show that they have names printed on the back of their shirts. The audience laughs and so does Geeky Al.

                    GEEKY AL
That clears it up. NOT!

                    GEEKY AL (yells to audience)
COMPUTER!!!

                    AUDIENCE (yells back)
GEEK!!!

                    GEEKY AL (to Red Team)
Welcome to the show, and good luck to all of
you. You are with the returning Champion of
five years in a row, needs no intro- TOM!

Audience CLAPS and CHEERS very loud.

                    GEEKY AL
Let's go meet the other geeks!

Geeky Al walks over to the BLUE team.

                    GEEKY AL(speaking to Tina)
Hello, team lead can you introduce yourself?

                    TINA
Yes, I'm Mr. Taylor. And it's a pleasure to be
here. I'm sure I have a great team.

                    GEEKY Al
Okie-Dokie then, please not so formal, first
names will do just fine. Next, same drill and
spill!

Geeky Al walks over to the first kid on the
BLUE team. MIMI, she has on jeans and blue
t-shirt, long braids in her, with blue beads.

                    MIMI
I'm Mimi, and I'm 10 years old, and I represent
the team spirit.

                    GEEKY AL
Good luck with that sweetie! Just kidding,
that's why you have all the blue on, Huh?

                    MIMI (she claps a beat)
Yes. BLUE-BLUE, Tie my shoe were gonna wipe the
floor with you!

The audience laughs loud.

                    GEEKY Al
Okay then, Little Ms. MAMA

Geeky Al walks to the next kid on the Blue
Team. CHUCKY, he's overweight, medium length
black hair to his ears, not hanging past his
shoulders in the back. He's wearing baggy
pants, and white t-shirt.

                    CHUCKY (very firm)
My name is Chucky, I'm 11.

                    GEEKY AL
Alright, let's hear it for Chucky.
Computer!!!

                    Audience (yell back)
Geek!!!

                         41

Chucky growls at the audience filled with kids.
Geeky Al growls back at Chucky in a silly way.
Audience laughs at Geeky Al.

                    GEEKY AL
Sorry no growling allowed, except by me
of course.

Geeky Al moves onto the last team member. STAR,
is a very petite girl, with long pretty blonde
hair, with a perfectly aligned bright smile.

                    GEEKY AL (smiling)
Last but surely not least, you know the drill.

                    STAR
I'm Star, and I'm the oldest on the team, so I
guess I will have to be the team assistant by
default. I'm 12, I probably have more
experience than my team mates, and I will try—

Geeky AL removes the microphone from in front
of her.

                    GEEKY AL
Excuse me sweetie, really that's enough this
isn't a beauty pageant. Oh! Did I say that out
loud? Just kidding, we all know why you are
here. To win!

                    GEEKY AL
There you have it boys and girls these are the
contestants for this year's Computer Olympics.
We will take a short break, and when we come
back we will get this party started!!

42

                    GEEKY AL (to Audience)
But first out of curiosity I want to know who
do you think is going to win? Just use your
touch pads in front of you and press the RED or
BLUE button.

Seconds later the results are displayed on the
digital board.

                    GEEKY AL
Wow, 99% says Red. That's brutal. You just
never know what you are going to get with a...
COMPUTER!!!

                    AUDIENCE (Screams)
GEEK!!

                                        CUT TO:

INT. BEAUTY SALON — DAY

Sara is watching the TV program with other
ladies in a beauty salon.

                    SARA (V.O.)
Oh my goodness, what is she doing, this was a
bad, bad, idea.

                    LADY 1
Now this is a positive thing for the kids.

                    LADY 2
About time they did something positive for the
kids.

                    LADY 3
For the past five year's it's been the same
Champion, hopefully that fat little man will
win this year, I'm tired of that same old guy
winning.

INT. BARBERSHOP - DAY

David is in the shop getting his hair cut.

                    BARBER
Hey, how does it feel to be the creator of a
hit game show?

                    DAVID
Just co-creator, Tom is the other creator. And
you know it feels good. I'm just hoping for
something a little different this year.

                    BARBER
Like what?

                    DAVID
For starters a new champion, I think people are
tired of seeing the same champion for five
years straight.

                    BARBER
Maybe the new guy will surprise us this year
and win.

                    DAVID
I think we need a surprise, something,
something different.

                         44

Chapter Seven

INT. PHILIPS ARENA - NIGHT

The games are starting. Tina is standing in a
huddle with her team on their side.

        TINA
Gigi, Bucky and Moon, listen up!
Only do what I say and I can win this,
well we can win this, if you do exactly as I
say.

        MIMI
My name is Mimi, not Gigi.

        STAR
My name is Star, not Moon.

        TINA
Star-Moon, what's the difference?

        CHUCKY
I'm Chucky, like that killer doll.

        TINA
Ooooh I'm so scared. You mean more like *Chuck
E. Cheese.*

Music starts, and the host comes back out on
stage.

        GEEKY AL
Alright boys and gals are you ready
to get this show started?

The audience SCREAMS, SHOUTS and CLAPS.

                    GEEKY AL
The first part of the game we will test
troubleshooting skills. In this part of
the game, team work will have to be strong.

                    GEEKY AL
To refresh everyone's memory there are three
parts to Computer Olympic Games. The
contestants will be tested on Troubleshooting
Skills, Technical Skills, and Customer Service.

The kids put on their headsets, and walk across
the stage to another stage setup that looks
like an office. It's filled with cubicles and
volunteers who are parents. The parents are
sitting in office chairs facing a PC waiting to
be told what to do.

                    GEEKY AL
Okay, this is how it works.
Parents are over there waiting in our stage
office setup for instructions on what to do to
solve a problem.

                    GEEKY AL
We have six parents, and three problems for
each team to resolve. Once the team corrects
the problem a loud ding will sound. And who
ever corrects the problem the fastest will win
challenge.

46

                    GEEKY AL
The team leads will have to lead their teams to
perform the correct troubleshooting. They will
only be able to speak to them via the
microphone/headsets.

                    GEEKY AL
You and everybody at home will be able to see
the problem and hear the discussions as the
problems are resolved. The scoreboard will
display the problem.

                    GEEKY AL
Red team, you guys go into the sound proof
booth; while the Blue team gets set up and
ready to go.

                    GEEKY AL
Blue team, if not completed in 4 minutes you
will lose the whole 10 points for the
challenge, four minutes on the board please.

The problem is posted on scoreboard for
audience, it displays "Printer Problem" The
BUZZER sounds.

                    TINA
What's the problem?

                    MIMI (to Parent)
What's the problem Ma'am?

                    PARENT
Every time I try and print it just sits there
and does nothing.

                    STAR (to Tina)
She can't print.

                    TINA
What happens when she tries to print?

                    CHUCKY (to Tina)
Nothing.
                    TINA
What is the printer doing?

                    CHUCKY
Nothing.

                    TINA
I need more details than that.

                    STAR
The lights are lit, and nothing is
flashing, and no messages are displayed.

                    TINA
Great! Make sure the printer drivers are
installed.

Chucky, Mimi, and Star all start talking at the
same time trying to tell the lady what to do.
She's confused and doesn't know what to do.

                    TINA
Hey, what are you guys doing? Time is wasting.
Just check to see if the drivers are installed.

Chucky, Mimi, and Star all attempt to talk to
the lady at the same time again, over talking
each other.

A loud buzzer sounds off.

Tina SCREAMS out loud like a girl. Everyone stops and looks with their mouths dropped opened.

> GEEKY AL
> Sorry folks, your time has run out! Now, it's time for the Red Team, to give it a try.

Tina gets angry and throws her hands in the air and SLAMS down on the podium.

> TINA (to her team)
> What were you guys doing out there? I thought you were smart!

> CHUCKY
> I thought you were a man! You scream like a girl.

> TINA (yells)
> What! Whatever, I'm here to win this money. Don't you guys want to win the money!

Tina's team responds at the same time by saying "yes" very low.

> TINA
> Let's act like it.

The Red Team starts the challenge. They are very organized.

> TOM
> What's the situation, guys?

                    Herman
The end-user can't print.

                    TOM
Sherman, you check the physical cables.

                    SHERMAN
Everything is in good, and set.

                    TOM
Verman, how are the drivers looking.

                    VERMAN (to Tom)
Reinstalling the drivers now... sending test
page... now.

                    HERMAN (to Tom)
Mission complete, Sir.

Time is stopped at 45 seconds. Loud DING sounds
off indicating completed goal. Audience CHEERS.

                    GEEKY AL
WOW! That was incredible! They displayed
amazing team work. This may be a tough team to
beat. Okay, the Red Team is leading with 10
Points and the Blue Team with zero.

Red Team goes into the sound booth again. And
Blue team gets ready for the next challenge.
The scoreboard displays the problem, "E-mail
Problem".

                        50

                    GEEKY AL
The volunteer parents will state clearly what
their problem is and the team will try and
solve the problem as quickly as possible.

Blue team is very eager to win this challenge.

                    TINA
You guys let's do this, show me how smart you
are, I know I am, just not too sure about you.
Show a little team work. I can't do it all by
myself.

                    MIMI
Can I do a cheer?

                    TINA
No, I hate cheers; I think people cheer when
they know they are going to lose.

                    MIMI
I cheered for my Mom when she—

                    TINA (interrupting)
That's great, I said no. Let's focus.

Two PARENT VOLUNTEERS are sitting facing each
other in front of their own computer.

                    GEEKY AL (yells)
Start the time, NOW!

                    PARENT VOLUNTEER 1
I can't send this email to my friend.

                    PARENT VOLUNTEER 2
I can't receive an email from my friend.

                    TINA
I hear the problem, what is the error message
from the one who can't receive an email?

                    CHUCKY
There is no error message.

                    TINA
Try sending a test message from that
account back to the same email account.

                    CHUCKY
Done.   Still no error message- nothing happens.

                    TINA
Delete all the deleted messages, and sent
messages; then clean up the inbox, if you have
to.

                    STAR
Let me do it! I want to do it. He's hogging
everything.

Star sits down, and slowly deletes everything.
Then Chucky goes and tells the other volunteer
to get up while he sits down in front of the
computer.

                    CHUCKY
I'm sending the email now to the other user.

                    TINA
Good.

                     52

                    MIMI
What about me, I want to do something.

                    CHUCKY
Go tell me if you see a new message sitting in
the inbox named "Test".

                    MIMI
It's here! We got it!

The alarm sounds the DING indicting the mission
completed within time limits.

                    TINA
Yes! I'm done.

                    GEEKY AL
Now it's the Red Team's turn. Can they complete
the same mission in less time? Let's find out.
Right after this commercial break.

Tina talks to her team.

                    TINA
You guys we pulled it off. Just pull it
together a little more, and I can win this!

                    CHUCKY
You can win this!

                    TINA
I mean, we can win this.

                    MIMI
Can I do my cheer now?

                    53

                    TINA
No. No. No! No Cheering.

                    MIMI
BUT-

                    TINA
And no buts! Concentrate on winning. Star, are
you ready?

                    STAR
Ready for what? Chucky does everything.

                    CHUCKY
Maybe if you didn't think about
how you look all the time—

                    TINA (interrupting)
Hey! Hey! Let's concentrate. And hope they
don't beat our time.

Commercial break is over.

The Red Team performs the same task at a faster
time. They received 5 extra points for
completing it faster than the blue team. The
Blue received 10 points just for completing the
last task within the time limits.

Chapter Eight

INT. PHILIPS ARENA - DAY

          GEEKY AL

The Red team pulled that off with a much faster
time, which has earned them kudos. The team
scores are now at 25 Red team and Blue Team
behind them with 10 points.

The audience CHEERS.

          GEEKY AL
We are now entering in the final challenge for
round one. Which team are you routing for, Red
or Blue.

The majority of the audience SHOUTS "Red".

          GEEKY AL
Now with all the contestants standing in front
of a computer, they all have the same problem.
They cannot get connected to the Internet.

          GEEKY AL
The error that they are all getting is "Page
cannot be displayed". Each team member has to
troubleshoot their assigned computer, and will
start at the same time.

Tina whispers to her team.

                TINA
I really need to win this money, so
let's do it.

                GEEKY AL
Everyone will be able to view all eight
computer screens at once on our MEGA Screen.
Each team member will receive 5 points if they
get connected.

                GEEKY AL
That's right kids; this means that the Blue
Team has a chance to win round one. All right,
this is it, let's do it!

Tom looks directly at Tina and points at
himself then points to his eyes and points back
at Tina indicating that he is watching her.
Tina just shrugs her shoulders.

The big digital clock on the stage is set. The
challenge begins.

On the Red Team, everyone starts immediately;
Tom is the first one to complete the task in 30
seconds. His computer sounds off with a loud
DING. Herman, Sherman and Verman are working
hard and fast.

Tina completes it in one minute. She looks down
at Mimi she has Pom-poms doing a cheer with the
audience.

                56

                    TINA
What are you doing? Time is wasting.

                    MIMI
I got a little stuck so I thought I would do a
cheer.

                    TINA
What?! If you don't get back to your computer!

Star finishes first, and then Chucky finishes
after her. None of the kids on Red team has
finished yet. Tina start's yelling to MIMI.

                    TINA
Come on! Come on!

Mimi is working hard and fast. Time is ticking.

On the Red Team, Herman, Sherman, and Verman
all finish at the same time, beating MIMI. The
audience cheers.

All three boys on the Red Team look at Tina,
and point to their eyes, and point back to her
indicating that they are watching her, just
like Tom did earlier.

Tina drops her mouth wide open. She yells out
at the host.

                    TINA
Did you see that? What's that about?

GEEKY AL

WOW! Yes I did see that! Incredible! The Red team are the winners for round one. So they will get to decide what the next challenge is for tomorrow.

GEEKY AL

We have three computer screens lit on the scoreboard. The Red Team will have to choose one of them not knowing the actual challenge. They will choose A- Customer Service, B- Programming or C- Web Design.

A 20 second count down is placed on the clock. The Red Team is talks among themselves. The buzzer goes off.

GEEKY AL

What will it be?

TOM

We will go with A- Customer Service.

GEEKY AL

I hope you guys really know how to talk your elders, because tomorrow we are taking the show on the road. You will be helping 55 and older adults.

GEEKY AL

So tonight you better practice saying yes Ma'am and no Sir. And since the customer is always right, they will determine who the winner will be for the second round challenge of the Computer Olympics!

Geeky Al walks to the front of the stage.

                    GEEKY AL
Good night everybody! Oh, I mean Geeks of
America.

Chapter Nine

INT. PHILIPS ARENA — BATHROOM — DAY

Tom's team is in the Men's bathroom. Tina is in bathroom stall.

>   TOM
> Guys this is going be like taking
> candy from a baby.

>   VERMAN
> No doubt.

>   TOM
> You see, they are weak. They may be smart
> individually, but their team leader knows
> absolutely nothing about being a leader.

>   TOM
> We are going to run, bike, swim,
> hike, and play tennis.

>   HERMAN
> Why do we have to do all of that, this is a
> computer competition?

>   TOM
> You are right! But do you know what baby
> boomers like I do? They are physically fit. In
> top shape, you have to be ready for anything!

>   TOM
> Tonight we start off with a run, followed by a
> hike.

Tom and his team walk out of the bathroom.

Tina comes out of the stall.

> TINA (V.O.)
> Sounds like a plan!

EXT. PLAYGROUND - NIGHT

Blue team is standing in a circle formation.

> TINA
> Team, looks like we are in for
> a good fight.

> CHUCKY
> Are you serious? Why are we here?

> TINA
> We need to be prepared for whatever may come
> up. Do you know what Baby Boomers like to do?

> CHUCKY
> What? They are old people they don't do
> anything. They sit around and fart all day.

Mimi and Star are laughing.

> STAR
> Mr. Taylor, I don't see how
> this will help. I need to get
> a good night sleep or my brain will not
> be able to function properly.

Tina thinks back to the day she got fired.

                              CUT TO:

INT. TINA OFFICE — DAY
(FLASHBACK)

Tina is looking at the picture of DYNO on her
wall.

BACK TO SCENE

          TINA
Okay-Okay, enough complaining we have to
get to the next round, and win. We all need
that money right?

          MIMI (jumps and cheers)
Yeah! Let's do it!

          TINA (claps her hands)
I need five laps from everyone. Let's go! Let's
go! Let's go!

          CHUCKY
Aren't you coming Mr. Taylor?

          TINA
Why? I'm in good shape.

She looks down at her fake belly.

          TINA
I guess it can't hurt.

She starts to run with them. She starts to sweat and the white makeup starts to run off. She's having trouble running with all the heavy fake fat, it starts to bounce all over the place. She stops. Mimi catches up to her.

                    MIMI
Um, are you alright Mr. Taylor? You are getting a tan and the sun isn't even out anymore.

Chucky and Star come by, stop and look.

                    Chucky
Hey, what's going on? You look darker.

                    TINA
It's nothing, it's just me. You know some people may get a little red or pinkish in the face?

                    MIMI
Yes?

                    TINA (breathing heavy)
I just get a little darker, nothing to worry about. Let me see a mirror.

She looks in the mirror.

                    TINA (worried)
Oh, that's nothing to worry about.

                                    CUT TO:

INT. GYM — NIGHT

TOM and all three boys are doing a cycle class. Lights are out and the bike wheels are moving fast. They are looking very focused.

                                        CUT TO:

INT. GYM - NIGHT

Tina and her blue team are in a Power Step class. The INSTRUCTOR is full of energy. She's dressed with bike pants and a cut off tank top over a sports bra.

                TINA
See, this here will teach you all the coordination that you will need, trust me.

                MIMI (to Tina)
I think my Mom takes a class like this.

                CHUCKY
This seems like it's for girls.

                TINA
No, no, Chucky, this is for real men. Trust me, I'm a man, right?

MUSIC starts, they are standing in front of their step.

                TINA
Just do what the instructor does and you guys will be fine.

                        64

Chucky steps on his step, slips and falls.

                    CHUCKY (he gets up)
See, that's what I get for trusting YOU!

                    INSTRUCTOR (yells)
And turn, and pivot, basic right, and turn, and
kick, now take it to the side!

Mimi is keeping up just fine. She is doing so
well that she starts to add additional moves.
Star is moving, just having trouble staying on
the beat.

                                    CUT TO:

INT. GYM - NIGHT

Red Team is now lifting weights in a body
building class. All the boys are looking strong
and focused.

INT. PIZZA RESTRAURANT - NIGHT

The Blue Team is sitting at a table waiting for
pizza, laughing and having fun.

                    STAR
Hey, Mr. Taylor, you think we got a chance?

                TINA
Sure, absolutely, I think you guys
are great. All of you held your own
with the workouts today. You guys will
do just fine. Try to relax and have
fun with it.

                Chucky
It's old people. We've got nothing to worry
about. Young always win against old.

                MIMI
Why do you say that Chucky?

                CHUCKY
Because it's true! We are smarter, faster,
healthier. There's no way we could lose. Right,
Mr. Taylor?

                TINA
Uh, right-right.

                TINA
Just go in there tomorrow and be yourself.
That's about the best advice I can give.

                MIMI
What if they don't like us?

                TINA
They don't have to like you, for you to
do your very best. I've learned in this world
that a lot people won't like you for the
craziest reasons.

                    TINA
          (she puts her arm around her)
You'd be surprised at what grown people would
do in life to just get what they want. So
before you have to start living behind a mask
in life, be true to who you are.

                    MIMI
Thanks Mr. Taylor, that's why I like you,
'cause you keep it real. I want to be just like
you when I get older.

                    TINA
          (looks down and away, ashamed)
You might want to hold off on that
thought.

                    MIMI
What? What do you mean? You rock!

Pizza is delivered to the table.

                    TINA
Let's just eat so you guys can get
home and get a good night sleep.

Everyone starts eating the pizza.
They all take pictures and joke around.

67

Chapter Ten

INT. TINA'S HOUSE - NIGHT

TONY is sitting in her living room, watching
TV. Tony is an old friend, who is also in the
Computer industry. He is 6ft, slim, with a
smooth dark complexion. Tina walks in.

                TINA
Excuse me but who let you in?

                TONY
No, the question is who are you?

                TINA
I'm working with Tina.

                TONY
Really, last I checked she got fired.

                TINA
She's been helping out with the Computer
Olympic Games.

                TONY
Doing what?

                TINA
How about, I let her tell you.

                TONY
Sounds good, I'll be right here when she
comes through that door.

68

                    TINA
That door?

                    TONY
Yes man, that door! What are you, crazy?

                    TINA (slowly walking away)
I just need to go to the bathroom.

                    TONY
Whatever man, just go! Oh, I remember seeing
your face on TV.

Tina gets to the bathroom finds a bottle of
water. She opens it and squirts the water into
the toilet.

                    TONY (he yells)
You know you don't seem like Tina's type. I
guess it's just the money. I guess at this
point she'll do anything, just to get her hands
on that money.

                    TINA
NO, we just work together.

                    TONY
If that's so, why is she at work and you are
here?

Tina undresses and wipes all the makeup off
fast as she can, and crawls through her
bathroom window; and comes back around the
front only to bump directly into Tony.

                    TINA
Tony, Tony why are you leaving.

                    TONY
Don't worry you have company
waiting on you inside.

                    TINA
No Tony, just let me explain.

He walks away and drives off.

Tina goes back inside and plays the voice mail
messages on her machine.

                    MESSAGE ONE (BEEP)
Ms. Taylor, This is just a reminder about the
30 thousand we will need to process the loan
application.

                    MESSAGE TWO (BEEP)
Hey, just letting you know that I
ran into Tony and he said that he got
the rest of the money for you... did you hear
me? He's giving you the money.

                    TINA
I heard you. Now he's not.

Tina thinks back to the day she got fired.

INT. TINA'S HOUSE - DAY
(FLASHBACK)

Tina and Tony are standing up hugging.

                    TONY
Just try not to stress.

                    TINA
I won't.

Tony and Tina stepped out onto the porch. Tony
grabs Tina hands and looks directly into her
eyes.

                    TONY
You know you need to find time to
Date. I know you are looking for the
perfect job, but what about the perfect
man.

                    TINA
Perfect man?! No such thing.

                    TONY
Perfect for you, a man to help you realize that
you are an inspiration to all who come in
contact with you. And someone who really
believes in your dreams.

BACK TO SCENE

Tina walks in her bedroom and looks at the DYNO
picture, hanging on her wall.

                    TINA (V.O.)
DYNO, it will be mine.

She starts to work some more on her software
development. Then she notices a scrapbook of
pictures of her and Tony. She stops working and
just reminisces about her and Tony's past while
looking through the old photographs.

Chapter Eleven

EXT. SUDIVISION - DAY

Geeky Al and both teams are present at a sub-division for adults 55 and older. Six homes have decided to participate in the challenge.

The residents in the neighborhood are out playing tennis, swimming, golfing, jogging, and there's a group of them riding bikes.

> GEEKY AL
> Welcome back everybody! In case you guys haven't notice this is a community for 55 and older adults.

> GEEKY AL
> The show is still going on live; we have the Red and Blue Teams here, ready to get the challenge started.

> GEEKY AL
> Here's how it works. Each of the six homes that are participating has different computer related problems. Whichever team completes all their assigned homes the fastest, wins this round.

> GEEKY AL
> Red Team, you will have the addresses of 100, 105, and 110. Good Luck!

                    GEEKY AL
Blue Team you will have the addresses of
113,117 and 120. Good Luck!

                    GEEKY AL
The houses were picked at random for
each team. You will have 15 minutes in
each home to complete the task. Red team you
have 25 points and Blue team you have 10
points.

                    GEEKY AL
With all that said, work hard and fast. Once
you complete the task, don't forget to ring the
Liberty Bell that has been placed outside of
each participating home.

Tina and Tom walk towards each other.

                    TOM
You ready to eat dirt?

                    TINA
If it's a mud pie with your face on it!

                    TOM
Huh?

                    TINA
That's right we are going to- whatever you are
going down, you and the three dwarfs.

                    TOM
I'm so scared. Where did you come from?

                    TINA
Same place you did TOM, same place.

                    TOM
What? Whatever, you could have never survived
in the environment I've been working in over
the past 10 years. I slaved year after year,
never to get my due credit until this year, and
it was all worth it.

                    TINA
Worth it! What do you mean- worth it?

                    TOM
My plan, it got rid of the dead weight that was
holding me back from getting a promotion to the
Director of IT.

                    TINA
Director of IT?

                    TOM
I forged documents for months now making it
seem like our department was over budget and
had to do some cuts and-

                    TINA (interrupting)
And you got rid of your biggest threat.

                    TOM
So not only we were under budget
but there is extra money to double
my salary, when I accept the new position.

                    TINA
Sounds like no one can pull one over you.

                TOM
NOooo, haven't you been listening. You have to
get up pretty early to pull one over my eyes.
My eyes are always wide open, wide open- wide-

                TINA (interrupting)
I get it already! Wide open, I think
you will be in for a big surprise when you
lose.

                TOM
I think you should tell me now, seeing that you
won't be winning.

                TINA
No, I think I will plan for the surprise
to be done in a big way, a way that only
someone like you can appreciate.

Geeky Al walks over.

                GEEKY AL
Teams let get this started, at the sound of the
gun, go find your first home to fix.

Guns sound off. Both teams start
running.

The Blue Team goes to their first house.
Chucky rings the doorbell. The door is open.
MS. WILLIAMS lives with her pet cat.

                CHUCKY
Hello, anybody home.

                    MS. WILLIAMS
Of course, come on in, I've been
waiting.

                    TINA
Hello Ma'am, thanks for participating
in today's game.

                    MS. WILLIAMS
I just need for you smart young folk to help me
download these pictures of my grandbaby.

                    MS. WILLIAMS
You know my daughter had been trying for two
years straight, and nothing. And finally, Boom!
One right in the hole, bulls-eye! I guess yaw
are a little to young to hear such things.

                    TINA
Yes, if you could just point us
in the direction of your computer.

                    MS. WILLIAMS
Why sure, it's upstairs.

They look upstairs and it's at least 20 steps
or more.

                    TINA
Let's go you guys.

                    MIMI (to Ms. Williams)
Why do you keep your Computer way upstairs?

                    MS. WILLIAMS
If somebody breaks in my house, I don't want to
make it easy for them to get the good stuff.
All the kids reach the top and Tina is
struggling behind in the heavy fat suit. No
computer is in sight.

                    STAR
Excuse me Ms. Williams but we don't
see the computer.

                    MS. WILLIAMS
Because you guys haven't made it to the
top yet, walk around the corner.

They walk around the corner and see another set
of stairs. Ms. Williams is walking so slow
taking one step at time, that it takes a whole
minute for her to make it to the 5th step.

                    TINA (to Ms. Williams)
Can we just go ahead and start the process when
we get up there.

                    MS. WILLIAMS
No, wait till I get up there. I don't
trust yaw young folk, yaw might mess
something up. And blame it on me.

They continue to walk upstairs. The kids come
face to face with a large tiger. Tina comes up
right behind them breathing heavy.

                    TINA
Hey, why did you guys stop?

Tina stops.

                    TINA (whispers)
Kids, don't move. Ms. Williams,
there seems to be a tiger up here
roaming around.

                    MS. WILLIAMS
That's Kitty she's my alarm system. She
protects all my valuables.

                    TINA
Can you give her a command, that won't get us
killed!

                    MS. WILLIAMS
Sure, Kitty...don't kill, do-

She coughs on the word don't. The tiger hears
kill and starts to attack and growl.

                    TINA (yells)
Hey, you think you can say it again!!

                    MS. WILLIAMS
Don't Kill! Don't Kill!

The tiger backs off.

                    TINA
We'll wait right here until you
catch up. It's not a problem, nope not at all.

They all sit down, waiting for Ms. Williams to catch up. Tina checks her voicemail.

                    MESSAGE (BEEP)
Ms. Taylor we have decided to give
you a week extension, if you give us assurance
without a doubt that you will be able to come
up with the money; still plan to meet us this
Friday at 8:00am.

Ms. Williams finally makes it upstairs. So they all walk behind Ms. Williams while she puts the tiger in a cage. The kids see the Desktop computer but not the monitor.

                    CHUCKY
Where is the Monitor?! Already!

                    TINA
Hey, hold up. Be nice.

She picks up a remote control, and a big wide screen drops down from the ceiling. The kids look up in awe.

                    MS. WILLIAMS
My eyes aren't what they used to be
so I had to get the biggest one they had.

                    STAR
I'll say she's got the MegaZoom 4000 Screen.

80

                    TINA
Ms. Williams, seeing that you got the latest
and greatest screen out, what
type of connection do you have?

                    MS. WILLIAMS
The fastest dialup available!

All the kids mouth the words "Dial-up".

                    TINA
Dial-up? Dial-up? Did you say, Dial-up?

                    MS. WILLIAMS
Yes! Do you have a hearing problem as
bad as your weight problem?

                    TINA
No, and the weight problem is just
temporary.

                    MS. WILLIAMS
That's what they all say.

The kids laugh.

                    TINA
Can we just get to these pictures you are
trying to download?

MS. Williams walks over and sits in her chair.
She pulls up the web site where her pictures
are located. She points to where she has been
clicking to get the pictures. Tina notices that
she has been clicking on the wrong thing to
download.

                      81

TINA (points to the link)
You are suppose to click on this, not that.

MS. WILLIAMS
Look how smart you are!

The liberty bell is ringing outside. All the kids run to the window and look out and see that the Red Team has finished their first house.

MIMI
We have to hurry.

TINA
Here we go.

The file starts to download. 10% shows complete, then 15%, all of the sudden the connection is dropped.

STAR
What happened?

TINA
She has Dial-up, someone tried to call her.

CHUCKY
This could take all day.

TINA
Ms. Williams, how about you see who tried to call you and give them a call, so they don't call back and interrupt our connection again.

                    MS. WILLIAMS
The handset is downstairs I'll
go get it.

                    CHUCKY
No, no! Let me, I'll run and go get it.

                    MS. WILLIAMS
Sweetie, it's sitting on top of my bed.

Chucky flies downstairs, he sees the phone
lying on the bed. He jumps on top of the bed
not knowing that it's a waterbed and goes
soaring high in the air.

                    CHUCKY
Aaahh!

                    MS. WILLIAMS (yells)
Did you find it?

Chucky lands back on the bed.

                    CHUCKY
Got it!

He runs back up stairs, and hands
Ms. Williams the phone. She checks the phone to
see who called.

                    MS. WILLIAMS(into the phone)
Hey Sally, no I didn't get the pictures yet,
I'm working on it let me call you when I do.

Tina starts the download process again. The
download process gets all the way up to 100%.
Then she clicks on the first picture and
everybody, SHOUTS, it's a picture of a baby
crying with her mouth wide open. The screen is
so big it looks like the baby could eat them.

                    TINA
Ma'am, looks like you are all set
here, do you need anything else?

                    MS. WILLIAMS
Yes, can you click on all of them
just to make sure that they all will open.

                    TINA
But Ma'am, it's 30 pictures!

                    MS. WILLIAMS
I know, but as soon as I say that you
can leave it will probably break again. So I
want to see all the pictures first. Please,
have a heart; I haven't seen the baby in person
yet.

Tina looks at her watch disappointed.

                    TINA
Ma'am, whatever you like.

                    MS. WILLIAMS
You guys are so nice, I hope you win.

Tina starts to go open each picture one at a
time. With Ms. Williams requesting to go see
some of the some pictures twice.

84

Tom rings the next Liberty Bell just moments later, indicating completion of the next home. The kids from the Blue team run to the window, and look out. The kids from the Red Team are smiling, and pointing and laughing.

                                        CUT TO:

EXT. SUB-DIVISION — DAY

The crowd CHEERING, and local high school bands are playing. Computer games and events are going on at the club house for all kids to enjoy for free. Plenty of food and snacks are being enjoyed, while they wait for the winner to be declared for this round.

                    GEEKY AL
              (talking into camera's)
Hey, with only one home remaining for the Red Team, the winner of this round may be declared very soon; back to you Jim.

Chapter Twelve

INT. NEWS STATION - DAY

          JIM
Here at the station, we invited some
of the kids who didn't make the final cut, to
ask them who they think will win the
competition.

          JIM (to Kid 1)
So, do you think the Red or Blue Team
will win?

          KID 1
The Red Team definitely, they are so
far ahead of the blue team, there's
no way they can catch up!

Jim places the microphone in front of another
kid, a girl.

          KID 2
I hope the Blue Team wins, they have more heart
than the Red Team.

          JIM
There you have it everyone. We will keep you
posted of the outcome.

                    CUT TO:

INT. DAVID'S HOME - DAY

David the other co-creator of the Computer
Olympics Games, is watching the report in his
home. He shakes his head in disbelief.

                                        CUT TO:

INT. SUB-DIVISION - DAY

Tom and the Red Team step into their last home.

An OLD MAN planning to have company over, wants
to watch a movie on his monitor, he has six
plasma wide screens in his house.

                    TOM
You insist on watching a movie on your monitor?

                    OLD MAN
Yes that's right!

                    TOM
Why! The screen is so much bigger on one
of your Flat Screens.

                    OLD MAN
I want to be close to my honey.

                    VERMAN
Honey!

                    OLD MAN
That's right! I said it. I'd show you a
picture but I don't want you to drool
all over her.

                    HERMAN
Come on! She's like what 65 years old?! I doubt
if there will be any drooling.

They all walked to his computer located in the
cozy sunroom. They turned on the computer.

                VERMAN (amazed)
Who is she?

A pretty picture of a woman is saved on the Old
Man's Desktop.

                OLD MAN
That's right! That's MY honey.

                SHERMAN
Hubba-hubba-hubba. She is nice.

                OLD MAN
Close your mouth. She's all mine.

                TOM
Alright boys, let's focus at the problem
at hand. You all got plenty of time for romance
lessons later in life.

The bell rings outside. The Blue Team finally
completed the first house.

                TOM
Alright boys let's hurry! They are on
the move. So what's the problem?

                OLD MAN
The drive won't open.

                    TOM
That's easy! You got a paperclip?
Two seconds, that's all I need.

The boys start roaming the house for a paper
clip, only to find a wall full of *HotWheels*.
It's a collection of *HotWheels* cars displayed
on a wall, to form one big *HotWheels* car. It's
breathtaking. Looks like it took a lifetime to
make.

                    VERMAN
Wow! Look at the cars!

                    SHERMAN (to Old Man)
That's awesome, how did you do that?

                    OLD MAN (shouts)
Now boys, you need to stay away!

Verman is startled and jumps back into the wall
of *HotWheels* and a domino effect knocks all the
cars down.

                    OLD MAN
Hot Dog! Put my cars back, right now!

                    TOM
Are you on morphine old man? That would take
days.

                    OLD MAN (frustrated)
You boys better get to picking them up. Don't
let me repeat myself.

                    TOM
You boys go ahead and start picking up
the cars, while I work on this Drive.

The Red Team starts picking up the *HotWheels*
and placing them back on the wall.

Then another bell rings and the Red Team run to
go look out the window watching the Blue team
run to the next house.

                    TOM
Hurry! Hurry guys, I can't lose!

Tina and her team hurry to the last house. A
physically fit lady, BETTY lives at this home.
Tina rings the door bell.

                    TINA (shouts)
Hello, we're from the Computer Olympics!

                    Betty
I may be old, but I'm not deaf, just
hold your horses!

Betty walks to the door and opens it. She's in
workout attire that shows her physical fitness.

                    Chucky
Wow, you look great for your age!

                    Betty
What little boy? You trying to be funny-huh,
how old are you?

                    Chucky
Uh, I'm 12.

                    BETTY
If you want to live to 13, you better shut that
trap of yours.

                    TINA (interrupting)
How can we help you today Ma'am?

                    BETTY
I need my wireless connection to work on
my PC so I can listen to some music
downstairs while I work out.

                    TINA
That seems easy enough. Show us the way.

Tina arrives at the stairs and can't seem to
fit through the door way. She turns left and
right trying to squeeze through.

                    STAR
Can you make through Mr. Taylor?

                    TINA
Yes, I'll make it just push me a little bit.

                    STAR
We all will push you on the count of
three.

                    TINA
Not too hard I don't want to fall down the
steps.

                    STAR
One, two, three!

Star, Chucky, and Mimi all pushed, just a
little bit, and Tina got stuck in the doorway.

                    BETTY
I have an idea.

                    TINA
What's that?

                    BETTY
How about we give you a push from the
other side.

                    TINA
How do you plan to do that?

                    BETTY
I have a little dog downstairs
and he could jump up on your chest to
push you down.

                    TINA
How big did you say your dog is again?

                    BETTY
Don't worry he's tiny.

                    BETTY
TINY! TINY! Here boy, here boy!

The dog Tiny comes to the foot of the stairs, and looks up and growls, Tina looks down and starts to whimper. The dog is almost the size of a horse.

> BETTY
>
> Attack! Attack!

The dog starts charging up the stairs. The kids start SCREAMING and running.

> TINA (SCREAMS)
>
> Aawwwwhhhh!

The dog reaches the top and jumps on Tina's chest and pushes her down. She passes out. The dog drags her across the living room, and starts licking her face. The white makeup comes off and gets on the dog's mouth and tongue. Tina wakes up and thinks that the dog is about to kill her as he drools over her while foaming at the mouth.

> TINA (SCREAMS)
>
> Aawwwwhhhhh!

> BETTY
>
> The kids and I are downstairs, we are almost done, and we will be up in just a second. Tina quickly realizes that it's the white makeup that has been licked off. She rushes to the bathroom, and finds some makeup and powder and quickly puts it on.

> TINA (V.O.)
>
> I hope this works.

The kids come running upstairs; just a second
later, the last bell rings outside of the last
house for the Red Team. The kids look sad. Tina
looks sick & weird.

                MIMI
I guess that's it-

                TINA
Naw! Really, you don't say. Do you feel like
cheering now? Huh?

                BETTY
Hey, that's enough of that, right now!
These kids did a great job. They displayed
great team work.

                TINA
If they are so great, and such a
team, maybe they can continue losing
the whole game, without me.

Chapter Thirteen

INT. LOCAL BOOKSTORE- ATLANTA, GA

Tina is sitting at a large table in the back.
Checking her e-mail, and she has a lot of
'money making' books on the table. David co-
owner of the Computer Olympics walks back to
her table. Tina doesn't have the man suit on
nor is the makeup on anymore, she dressed in
jeans, and a t-shirt.

          DAVID
Hey, do you mind if I sit here?

Tina looks up at him.

          TINA
Nope. Not at all...

          DAVID
Hey, I know you. Remember me?

          TINA
Yes, the technical guy for the Computer
Olympics.

          DAVID
I have a confession; I'm really one of the
owners.
          TINA
Really! What made you do something like that?

                    DAVID
I decided to take an interest in our future,
and the best way to do that is taking an
interest in kids.

                    TINA
I guess that really helped you
out financially.

                    DAVID
No. The money is for the kids. Kids get the
short end of the stick when it comes to getting
a college education. I don't want them to find
out like I did...

                    TINA
Find out what?

                    DAVID
That the government helps only the really under
privileged kids. What about the kids whose
parents are middle class. It can be tough for
parents to make ends meet and save money for
their kid's college fund.

                    TINA
I guess you're right.

                    DAVID
I don't know your story, if it was
a struggle or not; but had to work a full-time
job while in college full time. This is my way
of giving back.

                    TINA
Why didn't you tell me, when I saw you
that day at tryouts?

                    DAVID
It's not about who knows what you are
doing with your life, just as long as you know
what you are doing will someday make a
difference.

                    TINA
Why is Tom allowed to be a player when he's one
of the creator's?

                    DAVID
It's a win- win situation. When he wins, he
donates the money to charity.

                    TINA
Let me guess, the charity of his choice.

                    DAVID
That's right, "Tom Kids."

                    TINA
I got you!

                    DAVID
Excuse me?

                    TINA
I didn't mean to say that out loud.

                    DAVID (he picks up her hand)
We can work something out, over dinner first?

                    TINA
No. I'm sorry. Don't get me wrong you are fine.
But I think I'm going to give my heart a try
with someone who it really already belongs to.

Tina is angry now knowing what Tom has been up to all these years. She is determined now more than ever to do what's right for the children.

INT. TINA'S HOUSE — MORNING

Sara is over Tina's house applying Tina's makeup as the phone rings.

                    SARA
Do you want me to answer that?

                    TINA
No, I know who it is.

The call is transferred into the answering service. The caller leaves a message and they listen while still getting the fat suit back on.

                    CALLER (message)
I'm to assume Ms. Taylor that not showing up for the appointment today, speaks volumes, in that you are no longer interested in the loan. Have a great day!

INT. PHILIPS ARENA - DOWNTOWN ATLANTA, GA - NIGHT

                    GEEKY AL
We are back Geeks! Ready to wrap this competition up.

98

The crowd is cheering, Mimi is leading a cheer
for the Blue team to win; seconds later TINA
walks in the Arena and on the set.

                MIMI
Mr. Taylor, you came back!

                TINA
YES, I'm sorry. I came to cheer you guys on to
victory.

                MIMI
Cheer, you don't think we will lose.

                TINA
No, forget what I said, I'm sure you can do it.

                TINA
You guys didn't need me all this time,
I was just along for the ride. I know you guys
can do it I'm just here for support, and to
give back.

                CHUCKY
To give back! We didn't give you anything?

                TINA
Yes, you did, and I'm here to make sure
you get what you deserve.

                TOM (interrupting)
Blah-Blah-Blah, are you here to play the game
or what?

                    TINA
Are you ready to lose?

                    TOM (he laughs hard)
Now that's a good one. You got crushed
in round one and two, and you honestly think
that you are going to come back in here and
WIN. You must be dreaming!

                    TINA
I was, now I'm awake, and still
dreaming. I'm dreaming BIG, bigger than you
could ever imagine.

                    TOM
Once again, Blah-Blah-Blah...

The music starts, the crowd is cheering. 50
thousand people waiting to see the outcome of
the game. Tina looks into the crowd, and sees
happy, young, and old faces.

                    GEEKY AL
Here are the rules for round three.
In this round only the kids will be doing the
work. The team leader can only advise the kids
what to do, if asked.

                    GEEKY AL
In this round the kids will be programming. I
will tell you what program to create, and you
will use the tools given to you to create the
program.

The scoreboard lights up with the first
problem.

                    GEEKY AL
Okay boys and girls, create a game program
that's sports related. For example, basketball,
golf, tennis, baseball. I'm sure you guys get
the point.

                    GEEKY AL
Set the clocks! 30 minutes is on the clock.
Good luck to both teams! While you wait try
your own luck at the PC stations we have set
up.

The buzzer sounds as both teams are working
fast and hard as possible. On the Red Team Tom
is really involved in the process. Tina is just
closely watching from behind, letting her team
do what they want.

Fifteen minutes pass and still no involvement
has been asked of Tina. She starts to get a
little nervous.

With minutes left Mimi turns around and ask
Tina one question. Tina writes down something
on a piece of paper and puts the pen behind her
ear. The buzzer sounds.

                    GEEKY AL
It's up to the kids in the audience. I need you
guys to place your votes.

The votes are tallied, and it's declared the
winner is the Red Team.

                    GEEKY AL
The winner is the Red Team!
Congratulations, Red Team.

Tina SHOUTS out. And at the same time grabs the
pen from behind her ear, she doesn't notice
that the pen gets snagged on her wig; and
throws the pen across the stage and the blonde
wig goes flying in the air with it.

                                        CUT TO:
INT. BARBERSHOP - DAY

Men are in the shop getting their hair cut and
men waiting for a hair cut.

                    BARBER (laughing)
                 (to everyone in shop)
It looks like David got his wish for something
a little different this year.

BACK TO SCENE

Silence comes over the crowd, as they all look
at Tina; with a net on her hair covering her
long black hair. After noticing what happened,
she looks at herself on the big screen she
takes her hair net off.

Tom, looks more surprised than anyone;
realizing that Mr. Taylor is none other than
Tina.

                    TOM (laughing)
That explains the white powder. I thought you
had just finished eating some white powder
doughnuts.

                    TOM
What in the world were you thinking? You
actually thought you would get away
with this?

Everybody is looking very disappointed and
surprised, especially the kids.

                    TINA
Listen everybody, I'm truly sorry,
for the deception, and just everything.
Most of all, I'm sorry for hurting the kids. I
still would like to make it right, if given the
chance.

David walks on the stage.

                    DAVID
I take it this was your little problem. Can't
say that I'm happy about how you went about
trying to solve it, but what do you have in
mind, to make it right?

                    TINA
I was thinking I could compete directly against
Tom. Winner takes all!

                    DAVID
That is an idea.

                    TOM
HELLO, I do have a say in this matter.

                    TINA
Tom, if I win I'll give my winnings to
the kids on your team.

                    TOM
And if I win?!

                    TINA
I guess you can do whatever you want
with your winnings. Perhaps give it to "Tom
Kids", or should I say to your summer vacations
in Hawaii.

Tom is now aware that Tina knows about the fake
charity. He quickly agrees.

                    TOM
Sure! Why not?

                  GEEKY AL
That was a weird moment for a second. Winner
takes all! The challenge is, who ever develops
the most creative learning web site for kids is
the winner.

                  GEEKY AL
Both of you take your places behind one of the
computers. Once again, the kids are the judges.
Set the TIME for 15 minutes please. GO!

The challenge starts. The crowd is looking very
intense and confused.

The challenge goes on for 12 minutes.

She thought about her own designs that she had
developed and changed them to cater to kids.
Her design was very kid friendly.

BUZZ!

GEEKY AL
Time is up!

Tina and Tom take turns demonstrating their web
sites to the kids.

GEEKY AL
Kids make your choice! Simply push your Red or
Blue button.

Moments later the scoreboard is lit up and
about to display the winner.

Music plays.

GEEKY AL (jumps up)
And the winner is... the Blue Team! The Blue
Team! The Blue Team wins it all!!

Tina starts an uncontrollable laugh.
Tom is staring her down with his arms crossed.

JOE
What are you laughing at?

                    TINA

That would be you. Just wanted to make sure you
get a good look at who's having the last laugh.

Mimi walks up to Tina.

                    MIMI

I told you, you rock... Ms. Taylor.

                    TINA

No. You rock. And don't ever let anybody keep
you from cheering. That's your spirit. It's who
you. Let it out, always!!

The crowd start's to CHEER for Tina. Mimi
starts another cheer for Tina. Everyone is
happy and CHEERING, except for Tom. The kids on
the Red Team still received $20,000 each, the
winnings from both team leads. And the Blue
Team received their full $40,000 and a
computer.

Tina told David about Tom's fake charity. Tom
decided to give the money back in exchange for
his freedom. David now has full control of the
Computer Olympics Games.

Chapter Fourteen

INT. TINA'S HOUSE - DAY

Tina returns to her house after doing some grocery shopping. Tony is standing at her door with flowers in his hands.

              TINA
Hello, Tony. I guess you saw, huh?

              TONY
That would be, yes! I think everybody saw that wig fly off your head.

              TINA
Pretty pathetic I know.

              TONY
That was pretty crazy.

They both walk inside of the house to find Roses everywhere.

Tina looks back at Tony.

              TINA
You, did this?

He nods. She goes to check her voicemail.

                    MESSAGE (Sara)
It's me, just thought it was time somebody else
help dress you. I left something for you in a
box. I think you know what to do with it.

She looks next to her bed and finds a small box
with a red bow. She picks it up and walks
towards Tony. She hands him the box.

                    Tony
For me?

                    TINA
Yes, for you.

                    Tony
I have something for you.

He hands her a small box. She opens it.
It's empty.

                    TINA
I don't understand.

                    Tony
The empty box symbolizes two things.
First, my life would be empty without you. And
secondly don't forget your dreams are always
too big to be contained in a small box. So keep
on dreaming big.

                    TINA
You are too sweet.

                    TONY
So are you. And you are deserving of a chance.

He hands her an envelope, filled with money, $30,000 dollars to be exact.

                TINA (as she looks inside)
What's this? Are you sure?

                TONY
More than anything in my life.

                TINA
You didn't open your box.

He opens the box and finds the spare key to Tina's house.

                TONY
Are you sure?

                TINA
More than anything in my life.

FOUR YEARS LATER.

Tina and Tony are married. Tina started a business named CHEER instead of DYNO, with the same cylinder designed building. CHEER is the #1 selling children's software company in the world.

Mimi became a cheerleader in High School. Chucky is heart throb and a star football player. Star, became homecoming queen. Different as they are they all have one thing in common, they work for CHEER, Inc. after school, including the triplet boys.

Also, someone was so impressed with the work that Sara did on Tina she moved to Hollywood to be the designer she always wanted to be.

FADE OUT:

Dear Tony,

It's been a couple of days now. I was just wondering if you got a chance to finish reading the story.

Dear Tina,

I must say that the ending is quite interesting, you know, the last scene with you and me, since it didn't happen.

Tony is sending her an email on his hand held device, sitting in Limousine, outside of her house.

Dear Tony,

Sorry about that, it's Hollywood, what can I say?

Dear Tina,

Come outside.

She walks outside and sees the black Limousine, tied with big red bow on top. She walks to the Limo, and the Limo driver gets out and opens the door for her. She's dressed with old jeans and a t-shirt. Tony is inside dressed in a black tuxedo. She steps inside and sits down next to Tony.

"Say yes, and we'll make that last part true,"
said Tony. As he opens up a black box that has
a Diamond ring the size of a dime.

He looks at her the same way he did several
years ago when he kissed her. She instantly got
that same safe feeling as she did years ago.
And knew that she was going to be loved and
taken care of like no other had tried before.

"Yes," said Tina. Confident that she no longer
has to fight battles on her own, and that she
has a partner for life.

Tony placed the ring on her finger, and asked,
"Now, where do you want to go?"

She replied, "It really doesn't matter,
I just want to experience you."

He simply replied, "I Know," and kissed her
that same way as he did several years ago.

ISBN 142511385-0